D0090772

SECOND IN COMMAND

Sandi Van

An imprint of Enslow Publishing

WEST **44** BOOKS™

Please visit our website, www.west44books.com. For a free color catalog of all our high-quality books, call toll free 1-800-542-2595 or fax 1-877-542-2596.

Cataloging-in-Publication Data

Names: Van, Sandi.
Title: Second in command / Sandi Van.
Description: New York : West 44, 2019. | Series: West 44 YA verse
Identifiers: ISBN 9781538382615 (pbk.) | ISBN 9781538382622 (library bound) | ISBN 9781538383315 (ebook)
Subjects: LCSH: Children's poetry, American. | Children's poetry, English. | English poetry.
Classification: LCC PS586.3 S436 2019 | DDC 811'.60809282--dc23

First Edition
Published in 2019 by
Enslow Publishing LLC
101 West 23rd Street, Suite #240
New York, NY 10011

Copyright © 2019 Enslow Publishing LLC

Editor: Caitie McAneney
Designer: Sam DeMartin

Printed in the United States of America

CPSIA compliance information: Batch #CS18W44: For further information contact
Enslow Publishing LLC, New York, New York at 1-800-542-2595.

This book is dedicated to military families who take care of each other and our country every day, and to my favorite sailor who always has my back.

WHEN WE WERE 10 AND 7

my little brother, Jack,
locked himself in the bathroom.

Our sister, Reina,
all drool and diapers,
wouldn't stop crying.
Mom's heart held
in her tiny fists.

Jack went in,
turned the lock,
said he'd never come out.

Never. Ever.

His voice a
thundercloud
and then
raindrops.

NEVER.
 EVER.
  Ever.
   You
    can't
     make
      me.

Dad left the ladder
propped against the house,

wet leaves in a clump
at its base.

I shifted it—
  slowly,
    carefully—
until it reached
the bathroom window.

Climbed up,
one cold
metal rung
at a time.
squeak
  squeak
    squeak

Looked in at Jack,
face pressed against the door.
Like he knew I would wait for him—
        knew I would come for him.

I tapped on the window.
        tap tap
I tapped louder.
        TAP TAP

Leo?

His voice
a single raindrop.

        It's okay, I said.
        I've got your back, I said.
        Always and forever, I said.

2

Now, six years later,
the pane of glass between us
is thick.
And he can't hear my voice.

If he could,
what would I say?

I'm not sure
I can rescue him
this time.

SCOUT OATH

We make the
promise
every week.

Honor.
Duty.
Help.

The words
forever
stuck
in my brain.

I will do
my best.

THE DAY MOM LEFT

Early in the morning—
so early
the darkness was a blanket
over my face.

Like when Jack and I
would build a fort in the family room,
hide underneath,
and eat bowls of salty popcorn.

You better clean up those crumbs,
Mom would say.

Today she says,
Goodbye.
I love you.
Take care of Reina,
and Daddy,
and each other.

Six months will go by fast,
I promise.

Then she kisses us each
three times—
once on the left cheek,
once on the right,
once on the forehead,
her lips like wet dough.

Leo,
she says.

Remember:
you're second in command.
I expect you to help out.
Toe the line.
Be Responsible.

I know, I say.
I will.
You can count on me.

Then she hugs Reina one more time
because Reina is cute and sweet.
And she doesn't have to worry
about taking care of the family.

And Dad,
who looks calm and
like he is about to cry
at the same time.

And we all stand on the walkway
while the sun tints the sky.
The ship waiting at the dock
is like an old-time painting.

Waiting to take
moms and dads,
husbands and wives,
daughters and sons
away from their families.

Families told to help out.
Toe the line.
Be Responsible.

Take care
of each other.

THE DRIVE HOME

We're minus one family member.
Jack and Reina sit in the back seat
already half asleep.
I'm in the front.

I swallow hard.
Keep my feelings down.

I'll drop you off at home,
Dad says.
Need to get to work.
You good with everything?
> *Breakfast.*
> *Kids on the bus.*
> *Homework after school.*

Don't forget.
I'll be back around eight.

I swallow again.
Nod.

Yes, sir.
You can count on me.

TRUSTWORTHY

You can count on me.
I'll carry the weight of us.
Our hearts connected.

THE FIRST 24 HOURS
ARE THE HARDEST

The house is empty,
quiet.

Mom's smell
whispers to me
like leaves in the wind.

I don't want to cry,
don't want to miss her.

But she is everywhere
and nowhere.

And I miss her
so much
it aches.

WHEN MOM IS HOME

we eat homemade rice and beans,
grilled pork,
fried plantains,
crispy and sweet.

We eat
until our bellies burst

Dad says he'll swing by
Taco Ted's.

Beans leaking from the paper wrapper,
salsa with no flavor,
limp lettuce that falls on the floor
as Reina yanks it out.

Maybe I should learn to cook.

CHANGE

Everything is the same.
Same classes, same kids.
But I am different.
I am alone.

Same classes, same kids.
They stare at me.
I am alone.
Can't escape the feeling.

They stare at me.
Like she is already dead.
Can't escape the feeling.
Emptiness like rocks.

Like she is already dead.
Everything is the same.
Emptiness like rocks.
I am alone.

THE PHONE CALL

My cell buzzes
in the middle of math class.

I ignore it,
but it doesn't stop.
> *bzzz*
> *bzzz*
> *bzzz*

Like a bee in my pocket
trying to sting me.

Excuse me?
May I?
Thank you.

I slip out into the hallway,
bathroom pass in one hand
phone in the other.

It's Jack's school calling.

Hello?
Yes, ma'am.
I'm his brother.
Yes, our dad works long hours.

No, I understand.
I'll be there at four.
He will.
Don't worry.

HOW WE HANDLE MOM BEING GONE

I prepare,
dig in,
help out.

Jack gets detention
for talking back.

WHAT JACK SAYS TO THE PRINCIPAL

It's not the same as the
truth.
It's what he thinks
she wants to hear.

What he thinks
we will all
believe.

> *I'm sorry.*
> *It won't happen again.*

Our mom, I start to say,
but stop.

The principal knows.
Everyone knows.
Those poor Solis kids—

    alone.

No mother to watch over them.
Dad gone all day.
It's no surprise
that boy
is acting out.

The principal looks at Jack,
at me,
at her desk.

Detention.
Apology letter.
I don't want to see you back here.

I nod. *Yes, ma'am.*
Jack nods. *Yes, ma'am.*

We all know
this isn't the last time
we'll sit in these chairs,
and say the words
like a song on repeat.

WHAT I SAY TO JACK

We ride our bikes home,
the wind in our faces
cold and mean.

Jack Attack, I say,
my voice a steam engine.

> *Yes, Leo Lion*, he says,
> his voice an angry growl.

I turn to look at him.

I've got your back.

You know that, right?

Growl.

Don't
push
it.

I DON'T TELL DAD

what happened.
He has enough
to worry about.

THE NIGHTMARE

Reina wakes up,
screaming.

I sit up in bed,
my ears full of her cries.
And I remember,

Mom isn't here.

It's okay,
I whisper into Reina's hair.
Her body shakes in my grip.

Dad's snores
fill the hallway.

You're safe, I say.
Mom's safe.
It's okay.

The nightmare
isn't real.

How do you explain to a six-year-old
that her nightmare,
a nightmare
of Mom dying,
isn't real,

but it could be?

MORNING RUNS

The sky isn't even pink yet.
The air is so cold in my lungs
it feels like fire.

I run.
The sound of my feet
a steady pulse
a heartbeat
a quiet drum.

Out here
it isn't me against
the world.
It is me and the world
united.

COMFORT IN ROUTINE

There is a peace that comes
after the first days
of emptiness
have passed.

A peace
that comes
with routine.

You've got this, I tell myself
in the mirror.

I hold onto the sink
to keep from falling over.

To keep from falling,
keep from shaking,
keep from showing the world
how I really feel.

Scared.

DOLPHINS

Reina comes downstairs,
her hair messy and uncombed.

Come here, I say.

She sits on my lap.
I brush out her long brown hair
until it's as smooth as water.

Part it down the middle,
braid each side,
the way Mom showed me
before she left.

      Take care of my baby girl, she said.

So I do.

I twist the ends
into her favorite hair ties:
pale gray dolphins
swimming around a rubber band.

      When's Mama coming home? Reina asks.
      How many wake-ups?

Too many.

Soon, I lie.

I tickle her cheeks
with the ends of each braid.

She grabs one and studies it.
Do you think she's watching the dolphins?

Maybe.
Do you wanna draw her a picture?
She nods and jumps from my lap.

I don't ask about her nightmare.

NOT EVERYONE CAN BE AN EAGLE SCOUT

That's what the scoutmaster
tells our troop
as we prepare
for the board of review.

It's not easy.
Meetings. Homework. Planning.
The mocking laughter that sometimes
follows us down the hallways.

But I live for the adventure.
The challenge.
The grit.

The new kids
are clumped
on the cafeteria benches,
their eyes bright and nervous.

You've got this,
I tell the boy next to me.
Pat him on the shoulder.
Smile bigger than normal.

You've got this,
I say again.
Remember the oath?

He nods.

Remember the law?

He says,
A scout is

> *trustworthy,*
> *loyal,*
> *helpful,*
> *friendly,*
> *courteous,*
> *kind,*
> *obedient,*
> *cheerful,*
> *thrifty,*
> *brave,*
> *clean,*
> *reverent.*

I smile and nod.

Remember the first aid we learned at camp?
He makes a fist with his hand
and then lets it go.

> *I've got this*, he says.

It feels good to help.
Feels good to be part
of a group.

When it's my turn,
the questions are hard.
But I've stayed up late at night,
flashlight under the covers,
handbook dog-eared and full of notes.

Life's plan
set out like a path of stones.

Walk on each one—
steady,
don't fall.

Eagle scout in the distance,
a large stone
waiting for me to step
firmly.

My future
wide open.

BEFORE SHE LEFT

Mom said,
You can be anything you want to be.
Look at me,
the only female chief in my department.

Don't let the world tell you
you can't.

Don't let the world tell you
they'll stop you.
Become who you were meant
to become.

And I will.

Each stone a little closer,
closer.

Steady now.
Don't slip.

THE APPLICATION

They tell us it's important
to have a goal.

To reach into the distance—
arms outstretched,
fingertips twitching,
eyes on the prize.

I want to help people.
Keep them safe.
Serve and protect.

I want to do the right thing.
Be the person that others
can rely on.

The first step waits for me
on the kitchen table.

Summer Youth Police Academy.

Mom's signature
in swirly black letters,
Dad's a single loop and line.

The pen hovers over the final space—
mine.

I am ready.

LOYAL

To be true—
faithful
to those in your charge
and those who serve you.
Loyal
  to God
    to country
      to family
        to self.

FRIDAY NIGHT

In the family room,
TV on mute
to silence the sounds
of gunfire.

Reina tucked safely in bed.
Dad's text: *Stuck late at the office.*

No Jack.

This is our thing.
Friday nights on the couch.
Eyes focused,
fingers clicking,
fighting the common enemy.

I text Jack again and again:
Where are you?
Where are you?
WHERE ARE YOU?

No answer.
I go on with my battle
alone.

AFTER MIDNIGHT

Asleep on the couch,
video game controller loose
in my fist.

The door opens.
Later, man, I hear
echo in the darkness.

Jack?

   Leo?

Where have you been?
I texted you.

    Sorry, man. Phone died.

He laughs, like it's funny.
Like my worry is a joke.

I'm only 16.

I didn't ask for this.

FACE ON THE PHONE

We sit at
the kitchen table,
Mom's face looking up at us
from Dad's phone.

How's Hawaii?
Dad asks.

>   *Good.*
>   *Good.*
>   *It's good.*

Three times.
Like she's trying to comfort
each of us in turn.

Her voice is upbeat
but her eyes are tired.

We miss you,
I say.
Try to smile,
try to hide the lump in my throat.

>   *Yeah,* Jack says.
>   *Leo thinks he's the boss now.*

I elbow him in his side.
He punches my arm.

Did you see the dolphins? Reina asks.

    Some swam by
    the ship last night, Mom answers.

She ignores the jabs
between me and Jack,
ignores the ghost in the room.

The ghost of her.

PRESSURE

Mom wants to know
how school is going.

How are my grades?
And Jack's?

Is Reina sleeping okay?
And Dad?

Mom wants to know
if I turned in my application
for the summer police academy.
When will I hear back?

And have I been
working out
and eating right?

I don't tell her
that Reina cries at night,
that Jack has been
sneaking around
and talking back.

I don't tell her
that I'm worried.
Worried I won't be
good enough
to get in.

And that I run
and run
and run

until the tears
on my cheeks
aren't from
the wind.

HELPFUL

Helpful.
Household chores.
Shopping, cooking, cleaning.
Weary from the weight of it all.
Service.

THE FLYER

A piece of paper pokes
out of our mailbox.
Bright yellow,
like it's trying to be
the sun.

I pull it out,
damp from rain.

Deployment Support Group
meets Tuesday nights at 7 p.m.
at the community center.

All families welcome.

SOMETIMES

the universe hears
when we think no one else does.
It knows we're alone.
Sometimes it sends us the thing
we never knew we needed.

X'S AND O'S

Mom filled out a calendar
before she left.
Wrote down who goes where
and when she'll be home.

Or at least when they told her
she'd be home.

Reina marks each passing day
with a big black X.

I circle the next few Tuesdays in red
and leave the flyer
on our kitchen table.

TUESDAY NIGHT

I convince the family
to come with me
to the support group.

Tell them I'll use
my lawn-mowing money
to spring for pizza
and sodas after.

Dad meets us there,
suit and tie,
looking tired.

Reina holds my hand in her left,
a stuffed shark in her right.

Jack drags his feet.

We are a postcard
of what gets left behind.

I'm looking around the room.
So is everyone else.

THE GIRL WITH BLUE HAIR

There are chairs in a circle,
like the way I picture an AA meeting:
Someone tells a story.
Everyone nods,
says the person's name,
thanks them for sharing.

There is a long table
with coffee and juice,
a package of cookies.
It crinkles when I pull two out—
one for Reina,
one for Jack.

They're in the circle
looking for a place to sit.
I slip the cookies into my pocket
and fill a cup of coffee for Dad.

That's when I see her.
A girl.
Hair blue like midnight.
Silver rings on each finger.
She smiles.

I stand
frozen
in
place.

THE TALK

You know the one.
Where Mom or Dad sits you down,
and tells you what happens
to your body.

The changes.
The feelings.

Where you find out
how babies begin.

Dad didn't know what to say.
So he sent Mom.

We sat on the porch
when I was 10,
and drank sodas.

She told me what to expect
from my body,
and what to expect
from girls.

But she didn't tell me
what to do
when my throat closed
and I couldn't even
say hello.

FROZEN AND THAWED

Jack sees me
standing there.
Frozen like a bird on ice.

Jack sees her.
His eyes travel back and forth,
back and forth.

Watches her find
a place in the circle,
follows.

Leo, man.
Over here.
I saved you a seat.

His hand pats the plastic.
pat pat
His left eye winks.
His mouth is full of silly grins.

The empty chair
is next
to her.

I walk,
boots full of sand.
Tell my mouth to open.
Speak, I beg it.
Speak.

I'm Jack, my brother says,
hand out.
This is Leo.

Nudge.

I stick my hand out.

Speak, please.

Nothing.

> *Shy, huh?* she says. *That's cool.*
> *I'm Zen. I think we go to the same school.*

STILL FROZEN

Zen.

I thought maybe
when she spoke
my brain would catch up.

Make words.

Instead a sound
like someone drowning
comes out.

Jack laughs.
I kick his leg.

Reina runs up
and climbs on my lap.

Hi. I'm Reina. This is Sharky.

Zen smiles.
Shakes Sharky's stuffed fin.

I like your hair, Reina says. *It's blue.*
Zen laughs.

Everyone can talk to her
but me.

WE'RE IN THIS TOGETHER

That is what the woman says.
The one in the pink sweater,
who must be in charge
because her chair
has cushions.

WHAT THE WOMAN IN THE PINK SWEATER DOESN'T SAY

It's okay to study a map.
To measure the distance
as it grows each day.

To watch their ship get closer
to the site of fear,
of dread.

It's okay to look at the sky.
And wonder if we'd know,
or if it would be quick.

Without warning.

It's okay to wish
that you could have gone
in their place.

AFTER THE MEETING

I'm not the only one
who thought to go out for pizza.

A group of high school guys
from the support group
high-five Jack
when we arrive.

He makes friends
faster than I can let go of
Reina's hand
as she heads for the arcade.

You okay? Dad asks.
His face hoping I'll say,
Yes.
I'm great.
Never better.

I nod.

We order.

Stare in strange silence.

A million years pass.

Dad puts his hand on mine.

Good.

SOLIS

There once was a family of five
that did what they needed to thrive.
While mom was away
they worked through the day
and prayed she would come home alive.

THE NEXT DAY

fills me with regret.
Pizza sits heavy in my gut.

I do extra push-ups

and sit-ups,
jog more miles
than normal.

I think about my spot
in the academy.

I think about all the things
that will come next.

And then
I think
about Zen.

Her hair,
her eyes,
her smile.

BROTHER

Jack looks tired.

When he comes downstairs,
I smell smoke on his clothes.
And something else.
Weed? He's only 13.

Who are they? I ask.
He shrugs.

>   *It's cool, man.*
>   *They're cool.*

Of course they are.
Of course they
aren't.

I think the words
but don't say them out loud.

Don't
do
anything
stupid.

AT SCHOOL

I look for Zen
in the hallways,
but the faces blend together.
Like someone's holding a filter
over my eyes.

I look for Zen
in the lunchroom.
Crowds in their usual places.

I eat with some guys from my troop.
We talk about our project plans.

What's yours? Dave asks.
I shrug.

My life an order of events:
        school
        summer academy
        Eagle project

The thread of family
woven through each one.

Day by day,
hour by hour,
moment by moment.

Never forgetting
what must come first.

THE FRIEND THAT KNOWS YOU ALL TOO WELL

You okay today? Dave asks.
You seem, I dunno,
somewhere else.

Dave and I met
at cub scout camp.

My mom got stationed here twice.
Good news for old friends.

We met at the shooting range.
BB guns.
Airsoft.
Archery.

I don't remember which one.

It was all about the target.
Eyes on the target, they would say.

Focus.

Now Dave hunts.
I stick to the virtual enemy.
The one on my game screen.

No blood.
No mess.
Not yet.

I'm okay, I say.
Up late, that's all.

My eyes scan
back and forth
across the room.

All the different groups.
It feels like we've broken
into smaller pieces.

Each group their own island.

Dave waits.
He doesn't believe me.
He knows there's more.

      Do you know a girl
      named Zen? I ask.
Giving up.
Giving in.
      Blue hair? Pretty?

Korean? he asks.
I nod.

Her? He points.
Laser-sharp eye.
Focused.

My heart thuds.

Her.

FRIENDLY

They say a scout should be friendly.
A skill I would like to improve.
It isn't easy for me to speak up,
and even harder to make the first move.

NAVY TOWN

She's new I think, Dave says.
Military.

It isn't a question
around here.
Families come and go.

The locals know
not to get too close.

Not Dave.
Maybe he knew I'd be back.

But we'll leave again
before I graduate.

Are they on the ship? he asks.
Is that how you know her?

       Something like that, I say.

Go say hi.

He shoves me out
of the chair.

It squeaks.
Loudly.

I'm trying.

PEOPLE STARE

I try to pretend
that no one saw me
fall out of the chair.

That when I look up
they will all be eating.

They will all be talking
to each other.

For two seconds
the room is quiet.

I feel their eyes on me.

Then the buzz returns.
And I am safe.

But not quite.

LEARNING TO BREATHE

Zen stands at our table.
I am still halfway between
the chair
and the floor.

She says, *Hi. Leo, right?*
I didn't mean to give you such a fright.

Oh gosh, forgive my constant rhyme
it doesn't happen all the time.

She breathes in
and out.

Hands above her head,
down by her side
shake, shake.

I'm Zen. From the meeting?
Sometimes I rhyme
when I'm nervous.

Breathe in.
Breathe out.

I think maybe you get
tongue-tied?

I stare.
Yes.

Try this.

She holds my arms,
lifts them over my head,
lets them go.

Deep breath.

In
and
out.

How about now? she asks.

I smile.
My brain finally works.

> *Thanks,* I say.

PART OF ME

Part of me
has a crush on Zen.

She's cute
and bold
and not afraid
to admit her flaws.

And she even
gave me her number.

Part of me
wants to be her friend.

So she can teach me
how to not be
afraid.

BACK TO REALITY

Lunch ends.
School ends.

Home waits for me.

What will it bring
today?

DINNER, PART ONE

Reina made dinner.
Mom's apron around her waist.
Tiny body propped on
the kitchen stool.

Sandwiches,
she announces.
Her voice proud.

Meats and cheeses laid out neatly
on paper plates.

Will you cut the bread?

    Of course, I say.

Kiss her on the top of her head.
Tighten the apron string.

Dad comes home early.
He grins when he sees
the sandwiches.

Pulls out a jar of pickles
from the fridge.
Made fresh by our friends
back East.

Reminds me of home, he says,
after he takes a big bite.

HOME

When you move
somewhere new
every few years.

When your family
is from a place
you've never seen.

You don't really know
where to call

home.

DINNER, PART TWO

We eat.

Dad tells stories
from his childhood.

He tells us how he came
to the United States from Cuba.
Alone and afraid.
How he was taken in by a foster family.

He tells us the story
of how he met Mom.

How he watched her play soccer.
Worried he would never have the nerve
to talk to her.

And thank God I did, he says.
Or there would be no
you,
or you,
or you.

He points to each of us in turn.

Jack laughs.
It's not the first time Dad has told
this story.
Not the first time he has lied.

*We know it was Mom
who talked first*, Jack says.

*When she kicked the ball out of bounds
and knocked the wind outta you.*

Dad grins.
Shakes his head.

We all start to laugh.

Picture Mom
in her soccer uniform,
mud on her knees,
smiling at Dad.

Saying she's sorry.

Man, do I miss her,
Dad says.

And we all stop laughing.

THAT'S THE THING

The moment you start
to feel happy.

Like everything is
going along
the way it should.

You remember
what's missing.

GOOD COP, BAD COP

I'm going out,
Jack says as we clean up.

On a school night? Dad says.
He looks at me.

Like I'm the one
who should be saying no.

Like I'm the parent here.
Jack's eyes meet mine.

I hear his silent plea.
Want to be the cool big brother.

The one who doesn't care.
The one who doesn't worry.

My mouth opens.
Closes.

Is your homework done? Dad asks.
Jack nods.

A lie.

Mom gave me her password.
I've seen his grades online.
Know he's falling behind.

I suppose, Dad starts.

       Math test? I say.
       Don't you have to study?

The air in the room is thick.

Some other night, Dad says.
Thanks, Leo.

Jack huffs. *Yeah, thanks for nothing.*
He storms upstairs.

How did we get here?

WHO DIED?

I knock on Jack's door.
Three times.
knock knock knock

Wait.

Nothing.

knock knock knock

Go away.

Wait.

*Who died and
left you in charge?*

Who
died
and
left
you
in
charge.

The words echo
in my ears
like gunfire.

TOE THE LINE

I speak into Jack's door.
He ignores me.

Can I come in?

What's going on with you?

*You're just mad
because you know Dad says yes
and Mom always says no.*

I'm not trying to replace her.

But someone has to be
the bad guy.

Someone has to
keep the peace,
maintain order.

Be Responsible.

INSTINCT

When you know your brother
will wait
for everyone to fall asleep.

Then he will do
whatever it is he does
to hold his heart
together.

MESSAGE

Back in my room,
I text Zen.

I want to tell her
what's on my mind.
Mom.
Jack.
And all the rest.

I want to tell her
how happy I am
that we met.

I want to tell her
she's pretty,
and I like her smile.

Instead
the text reads:
What's up?

WHO WE ARE

We text
back and forth
in the idle way
people do.

She asks about
my family.

I ask what
it's like
at her house.

She's an only child.
No one to watch over.
No one to worry about.

No one to wait with her.

It's her dad
who's gone.

Mom works part-time.
Home every night.

They watch TV together
and do puzzles.

It sounds nice.
But Zen says she is lonely.

People tease her
about rhyming when she's nervous.

I like it, I tell her.

>   *You don't think I'm weird?*

Of course you're weird.
That's what I like.

She laughs, *Hahahaha.*

I tell her about Jack.
Say he's on a bad path.

She tries to tell me
it will all work out.

Maybe it's for attention.
Maybe he's hurting.
Be a big brother.

It's what you do well.

COURTEOUS

When you see someone
struggle to open a door
or cross the street.

You hold out your hand.
You help them out.
It's what you do.

It's what you do well.

I KNEW THIS
WOULD HAPPEN

Jack is not in his room.

Window open.
Cold air.

Cold air
in my bones
like ice.

Like that time we camped
on the frozen lake.

Bodies tucked into
zero-degree sleeping bags.
Listening to the wind
howl against
our tents.

Jack's first year in
boy scouts.
His only year.

Leo, man, it's not for me.

He called me that
even back then.

When I was only 14.
Barely a man.

I knew I wanted to stay
in scouts.

Knew being outside,
being connected,
was where I belonged.

I wanted my brother
to feel that, too.

Wanted us to be
together.

Wanted to keep him
under my wing.

WONDER

I wonder where
my brother went.

Wonder what mess
I'll need to clean up
tomorrow.

IT WILL ALL WORK OUT

Sleep doesn't come.
It mocks me
with its promises.

I didn't tell Dad
that Jack left.

I didn't try to find
my brother.

Zen said
it will all work out.

Her words roll in my head
like loose marbles.

IN THE MORNING

We are all fine.
A happy family
minus Mom.

Eating eggs,
leftover ham,
black coffee.

Me.
Dad.
Reina and Sharky.
Jack.

Two of us look like
we've been up
all night.

NOT NORMAL

There is a rough edge
to Jack.

As if someone scraped
his skin away.
And now the bones
are free to feel
the fresh air.

I want to ask him
where he was.

Does Dad see the
way Jack's fingers
twitch?

Does he see the
darkness
under my eyes?

Something
isn't
right.

Am I the only one
who feels it?

7TH FLEET

Dad reads the paper
every morning.

Shares the comics
with Reina.

Gives the sports section
to Jack.

I study the
obituaries.

Not because
I like to
think about
death.

I like to
think about
life.

What did each person
leave behind?

What made them
who they were?

Today,
we all focus
on the front page.

Headlines
about the conflict
in Asia.

The 7th Fleet:
Ships, aircraft,
and personnel
that monitor
the Pacific Ocean.

The 7th Fleet:
Ready to respond.

The 7th Fleet:
Mom.

INNOCENCE

Reina does not
understand
words
like nuclear
and
missile
and
threat.

I want to be
that
innocent.

OPERATIONS SECURITY

Dad must read our minds.

Your mother is fine,
he says.

I talked to her last night.
She can't say much.
You know, OPSEC.

We know.
Operations Security.

It means Mom can't talk
about where she is
or what she is doing.

Because
it could put her
in danger.

It could put us
in danger.

I read the headline again.

There are forces
beyond our control
that could put the
world
in danger.

WORDS LEFT UNSAID

Jack slams his plate
in the sink
and mumbles something
under his breath.

Dad says not to swear
in front of Reina.

Jack looks at me,
waiting.

We can't just sit here,
he says.

Dad shakes his head.

> *There's nothing
> we can do.*

Maybe not there.
But here.

I have no idea
what Jack means.

But I am
afraid
to ask.

FEAR

We all leave the house.
And I can't shake the feeling
that something is wrong.

THE OTHERS

I sit on the bus,
head pressed against
the window.

Think about the others.
Other kids who miss their
mom or dad.

Our town is full
of them.

Sometimes you can tell
by the look in their eyes.
The sadness that grows
like mold.

Sometimes you can tell
by the clothes they wear.
Red, white, and blue.
Pride in our country.

Mostly you can tell
by the stiffness
in their spine.
The way
they seem
to be
always
on
alert.

WHAT HAPPENED

At school,
police cars are
parked out front.

I look for Dave
and find him
near the flagpole.

Wind whips the flag.
Makes a snapping sound.

What's going on? I ask.
He shrugs.

We file into school.
The uniforms make me
stand straighter,
walk taller.

Yellow caution tape
lines the hallway.

The science lab,
someone says.

Whispers turn to shouts.

Teachers work to calm
the students.

They try to prevent chaos
from snaking through
the hallways.

A crowd gathers.

Dave and I get closer,
closer,
until
I see it.

I see
what happened.

SOMEONE SMASHED THE BEAKERS IN THE SCIENCE LAB

Tiny bits of glass
break the light
into a million
sparkly pieces.

Each one speckling
the smooth black tables.

Liquid spills
down
onto the
floor
in quiet
rivers.

The policeman
in the doorway
stands silent.

The crowd behind me
builds.
>   *What the—*
>   *Who did—*
>   *Ah, man—*
>   *Someone's gonna fry.*

The door swings on its hinge.
It makes a sound
like a distant swing set.

Pieces of the glass window
form a pattern
near our feet.

Blood.

There is blood in the glass.

Whoever did this
will be found.

Whoever did this
will pay.

VOICES

The voices shout.

Step away, step away.

Get to class.

Move along.

Teachers.
Police officers.
Hall monitors.

Voices
of
authority.

Keeping us safe.
Keeping us in the dark.

A QUESTION

School
is where
you go to
feel safe.

But what
happens when it
becomes a
place of fear?

KIND

I will be the person
who makes sure
no one is cut by the glass.

Who offers to help
calm other students down.

I will not be the person
who stares and points.

Who looks at classmates
and wonders
which one
of them
is guilty.

WHAT HAPPENS NEXT

We are called down
to the office
one by one.

To find out
who knows
anything.

To find
clues.

Someday
I will be the one
asking questions.

I will be the one
fighting for justice.

WHAT I LEARN

Whoever did this
had a reason.

A purpose.

There are chemicals
missing.

Words whispered
in the hallway.

Bomb.
Attack.
Terror.

Panic
swims in the air
like a shark.

WHAT IF

No.

I cannot
allow myself
to think it.

EVERYONE IS QUIET TONIGHT

We sit in a circle
in the family room
folding laundry.

Mountain of socks
like a campfire at the center.

Reina wears Dad's pajama bottoms
on her head.
Always the clown.

Someone, I start.
Someone
broke…

My eyes meet Jack's.

He looks away.

Shoves his hands
into his pockets,
stands up.

Broke what? Reina asks.

Her pajama bottom pigtails swing
back and forth
between me and Jack,
me and Jack.

Jack backs out of the room.

Broke what? she asks again.

Nothing, I say.

WHY WOULD YOU LEAVE?

If you had
nothing
to
hide.

ARGUMENT

My gut says:

>   Follow your brother.

>   Confront him.

>   Find out
>   what
>   he knows.

>   If he was
>   involved.

My heart says:

>   Leave him be.

>   Trust him.

>   You're jumping
>   the gun.

The noise is too
loud.

My brain
can't decide.

TRIO OF SADNESS

Leo?

Reina's voice
breaks the chaos
in my head.

Broke what? she asks.
A third time.

I don't want to lie to her.

      Listen, I say. *It's okay.*

I pull her onto my lap.
Take off her pajama hat.
She leans her head into me.

      Someone at my school
      went into the science lab.
      They weren't supposed to.

      Glass broke.
      It wasn't
      safe to walk.

Are you okay? she asks.
Her eyes like big, round buttons.

I nod.
Is Jack? He looked mad.

I hold her close,
smell the apple shampoo
in her hair.

> *He misses Mom.*
> *That's all,* I say.

Me too.

> *Me three.*

MOM WOULD KNOW WHAT TO DO

She is the one
who keeps us
on the straight
and narrow.

THE BEACH

The first time we lived here
it was just me and Jack.
No Reina.

Mom and dad took us to
a beach along the Sound.
Let us stick our toes
in the cold water.

We chased scurrying crabs.
Ran our fingers along
the backs of sea stars.
Watched clams disappear
down sandy holes.

Jack walked further down
the tide pool.

I watched his tiny body
hunch over the water.

He shouted for me to come over.
To see what he had found.

I followed his finger.
Jack had spotted a sea urchin.
Shiny black spikes in every direction.

He wanted to touch it.

Mom had told us it was okay
to touch the animals.
Two fingers, she said,
and be gentle.

Jack's fingers stood ready,
his face lit with joy.

Isn't it cool? he asked me.
   It looks kinda sharp, I said.
   Maybe we shouldn't touch it.

Jack reached into the water.

I didn't know much about
poison.

But I had enough sense to know
the animal didn't want to be
touched.

I grabbed my brother by the waist
and pulled him away.

We both fell into the water
with a splash.

Boys! Mom yelled.
Rushed over to us.

Jack began to cry.
Mom took him in her arms.

She looked at me,
her face anger and punishment.

Leo? she said.
Waited for an explanation.

I could have told her
I was trying to keep him safe,
to keep him from getting hurt.
Could have told her about the sea urchin.

But I didn't.

> *I'm sorry*, I said.
> *It was just an accident.*

Just an accident.

OBEDIENT

To follow the rules.
To do what I'm told.
To stay on the path.
To maintain order.
To mind my manners.
To wait my turn.
To step up.
To keep in line.
To obey.

SUPPORT GROUP

Tuesday comes.

Worries about Jack
leave my mind
if only for a quick second.

Not as if things are calm
in a group waiting
to hear from their families.

People sit
on the edge
of their chairs
like dogs
waiting for
a treat.

A treat that
may kill them.

Zen pats the chair next to her.

As if we'd been
coming here
for weeks.

As if we've settled into
the way things
always go.

Can you believe what happened at school?
Whoever did it must be a fool.

To risk getting caught—
such a shame.
Do you think they'll figure out
who's to blame?

She smiles.

Her fingers find my arm.
A gentle squeeze
wakes my body
in new ways.

It takes time
to find my voice.
The fear of truth
in my throat like a stone.

My brother laughs
with his new friends.

Whispers.
High fives.

It doesn't take much
for it all to sink in.

Zen waits.

    Yeah, I say.

One word.
All I can breathe out.

Pink sweater woman
claps twice.

She's in blue today.
American flag pinned over her heart.

Let's begin, she says.

AFTER THE MEETING

I am not the only one
who put the pieces together.

When we get home,
cop cars line the street.

VISITORS

Two officers follow us
to our front door.

I want them
to be there
for me.

To tell me I made it into
the summer academy.

But they are not
here for that.

They are here to search.

THE SEARCH

The officers search.

Dad follows.

He tries to stay quiet.

They spend a long time
in Jack's room.

I see the veins in Dad's arms
throb with blood.

His face a rosy red.

Jack's face is white.

SENT AWAY

Leo.

Dad's voice.
Somewhere between
a whisper
and a growl.

Take Reina for ice cream.

He hands me the keys.
I only have my permit.

      But, Dad.

Go.

SMALL TALK

I don't want to
talk about dolphins.
Or sea turtles.
Or sharks.

I want to know
what my brother
is hiding.

THE WAY IT SHOULD BE

Reina and I drive home.
Knuckles on the wheel,
white with dread.

I pretend
it is all okay.

Imagine
it is all okay.

HOME

Sirens spin
in an endless pattern:

red
blue
red
blue.

A shadow steps
onto our front porch.

Hands on Jack's shoulders,
large and strong.

The moment swirls
around me
like a snowstorm.

FAMILY DAY

I remember
when Mom took us
on her ship.

Family cruise day
aboard the
aircraft carrier.

The ship
a city
in itself.

Jack had a toy plane
that zoomed through the air
to the sound of his buzzing lips.

Reina gurgled
in her baby carrier
and pulled at Dad's hair.

I took it all in.

The tight spaces
and narrow
stairways.

Voices that
rose above
the steady sound.

The smell—
like Mom's hugs
when she came home.

I thought about all the sailors.

Wondered where they slept.
What happened when they went to the bathroom.
Wondered if the ocean made them sick.
Where the food came from when they were out to sea.

Any questions? Someone asked.

Yes.
Yes.
Yes.

But I was too shy to speak up.

QUESTION

I only have
one question now.

A question for Jack:

Didn't you know
you'd get caught?

THEY'RE TAKING MY BROTHER AWAY

Dad's in the doorway.
Body propped
against the wood
to keep from falling over.

Reina half asleep.
Eyes blink slowly.
Colored lights reflect
onto her cheeks.

I watch
as my brother
enters the back seat
of a police car.

DOES IT?

I wait.

Wait for the cops to leave.
Wait until Dad slinks back inside.

Does that make me a coward?

INSIDE

Dad paces back and forth.
His feet a ticking clock
against the floor.

They took him in,
he says.
No prompt from me.

They took him in
for questioning.

Questioning.

Questioning.

Three steady beats.

      Do they think—? I start to ask.

But I know.
I already know.

They think he had
something
to do with the science lab.

      Did they—what did they find?

Dad stops.

His words spill out
in slow drips.

They
found
chemicals
in
his
room.

They
think
he—

They
think
he
plans—

Oh God.

My son.

How could he?

AT LEAST ONE OF US WILL SLEEP TONIGHT

I bring Reina to bed.
Tuck her in.
Kiss her forehead.

She shifts,
sighs,
falls deeply
into
sleep.

FIGHT

I don't know
what else to do.

So I grab the
game controller
and shoot.

I shoot
and shoot
and shoot.

Anger spilling out of me.
Sweat spilling out of me.

My fingers like
fireworks.

The sounds
in my headset
drown out
the sounds
in my head.

Dad's words.
His boots on the floor
as he paced.

Jack's laughter.
Plotting with his friends.

I should have known
it wasn't
innocent.

I should have seen this coming.

MORNING

The day starts.

Dad's gone.

Reina's in the kitchen
buttering her toast.

Sharky's in the place
where Jack should be.

Then I remember.

My brother
is
locked
up.

CHEERFUL

It isn't enough
to smile
through the pain
of Mom being gone.

It isn't enough
to pull my lips back,
bare my teeth.

Tongue pressed.
Adam's apple
firm in my throat.

I must dig deep,
find the joy.

For Reina's sake.

But the joy sinks
deeper
with every passing day.

The weight of Jack
pulls it
low
down
into
a place
with no light.

MESSAGES

To Dave:
Cover for me.
I'll explain later.

To Zen:
Meet me after school
outside the gate.
I need your help.

To Jack:
(Even though I know
he won't see it.)
Jack Attack.
I'm on my way.

POLICE STATION

I sign in.
Explain who I am.

They know.
Dad left an hour ago.

He thought I'd be by
to work things out.

That's what the cop says:
Your father said
you'd be able
to work things out.

Work what out? I want to ask.
        I can talk to him?
        My brother?

The cop nods.

Follow me.

We'd like a confession,
see who else is involved.

But he's not talking.
Think you can loosen his tongue?

Loosen his tongue.

As if it is tied into a neat knot.
And I have magic fingers
that know how to work it.

How to pull and pull
until the words come out.

My palms itch.

Sweat walks down
my back
in a straight line.

I'll do my best.

PROMISES, PROMISES...

They lead me to a room.
Rows of chairs
tucked neatly into
separate places.

Like when we had
to take tests
in middle school.

Smiley faces scribbled
on the cardboard.
Sometimes worse.
Crude pictures.
Words I learned
on the bus.

I sit.
Jack watches me
through thick glass.

How has it come to this?

We speak to each other
on strange phones.

No way, he says.
As if we were
in the middle
of talking.

They told me to do it.
Told me it'd be okay.

Nobody said anything
about a b—

The missing word
hangs in the air,
invisible.

It wasn't me, Leo.
I swear.
You've gotta have my back.

You promised.

...SO HARD TO KEEP

My mind flashes back

to the day
with the ladder.

When Jack refused
to face life
with a younger sister.

How simple it was then.

How easy to say the words,
with no need to worry
about backing them up.

WHAT I GET FROM JACK

Yeah.

He was there
that night.

The night he and
the other boys
broke into the lab.

Boys from
our support group.

Their support in the form
of terror.

Jack wasn't forced
to join them.

But he was forced to
hide what they stole.

He swears he didn't know
the plan.

I don't believe him.

But he is my brother.

And I promised.

WHAT IF

What if I cover for him
and he is lying?

What if the scoutmaster
learns what I did
and kicks me
out of the troop?

What if the cops
ban me
from the one
thing
I want
in life
more than
breath?

RESPONSES

I leave the station.
Check my phone.

Dad wants to know
if I went to see Jack.

Don't skip school, he wrote.
But make sure he's OK.

As if I could somehow
do both.

Dave sent a thumbs-up.

Zen sent a concerned face
and the words: *I'll be there.*

I feel less alone.
But not less afraid.

3 P.M.

She stands
outside the school gate.

The blue in her hair
like the deep ocean
on a sunny day.

For a moment
I forget
why I asked
her to come.

UNKNOWN REASONS

Oh Leo, Zen says.

Her head tilts the way
Mom's would
when we spilled
our cereal
on the floor.

Is everything all right?

She reaches for my hand.
Takes it in hers.

     I—we—Jack—

Words jumble in my brain.

I close my eyes
and try to sort them all out.

     The lab, I say.

Eyes open.

     It was Jack.
     And the guys, ya know,
     from group?

Her mouth is an O.
She nods.

Knows exactly who I mean.

Why?

I shrug.
The answer an itch
I don't want to scratch.

THRIFTY

Conserve.
Be careful.
Use only
what's
needed.

Use
only
what's
needed.

THE NOTE

Zen releases my hand.

Reaches into her pocket.
Pulls out a piece of paper.
Crumpled lines smoothed straight
and folded into a neat square.

She stays silent.
Passes me the paper.

I am afraid of what
will happen
if I read it.

But more afraid of what
will happen
if I don't.

WORDS THAT HURT

Zen speaks.
Her voice quiet
and shaking.

*I found it
in my locker.*

Her eyes stare down
at her feet.
Toes tap nervously.

I unfold the square.
Read.

Words of hate.
Words of fear.

Slang against Zen
for who she is
and where her family
came from.

> *Are you the only one?* I ask.

She shakes her head.
She saw other notes.

On the ground.
In the trash.

Other students,
Asian, like her.

Huddling in corners
sharing their crumpled slips.

Now it is my turn to ask.

Why?

QUILT

We are all a part
of a unique people quilt.
Some of us believe
in the beauty of it all.
But some choose to live in fear.

STUCK IN MY MIND

I don't want to accept
the truth.

My brother's theft,
the letters left,

are connected
in hatred.

THE ONLY THING TO DO IS LEAVE

My defenses are up.

The big brother in me,
the one who promised
to protect,
steps in.

No way, I tell Zen.

Her eyes meet mine.

*No way
my brother
would use
those words.*

*Our dad—he's from Cuba.
He taught us to accept everyone.*

Jack's not to blame.

*He'd never call you
those horrible things.*

Zen starts to cry.
Tries to speak.

But I don't stick around
to listen.

I RUN

And run
and run
and run.

Because that's
what my body
does
to feel
okay.

HELP

I want to call Mom
and tell her
what's happened.

To ask if
she thinks
Jack is
innocent.

But communication must be down.

Her phone goes straight
to voice mail.

There are no new emails
for any of us.

*Sometimes they do that
to protect us,* Mom said
before she left.
Don't let it worry you.

But right now,
in this moment,
with fear at my face
like a cold wind,
all I do
is worry.

DOES ANYONE KNOW?

What it means to be safe?
Protected?
Kept from harm?

THE HOUSE IS QUIET

Too quiet.

Dad is at work.
Because that is how
he keeps the family
together. (I never
understand what he
means when he says that.)

Reina's at her friend's house.
Because that is where
we sent her to keep her
safe (and in the dark).

Jack is at the police station.
Because that is where
people go when they
don't know how to behave.

Me.
All alone.
Trying to figure out
what went
wrong.

ASK FOR FORGIVENESS

The things I said to Zen
echo in my head
like fireworks.

I dial her number,
hands shaking.

Voice mail.
The need to talk to someone
grows inside me.

A beast
needing to be fed.

Zen. It's Leo.
I'm
so
sorry.

Call me.

THE FIRST CALL

My phone rings.
A number I don't know.

The station?
Jack?
Did he confess?

One of the three.

Leo Solis? A voice asks.

    Yes? This is him.

*Hello, yes, I'm calling to follow up
on your summer academy
application?*

    Yes? I say again.

My voice sounds
strange,
unknown.

*Right, everything looks good.
We'd like you to come down
to the station
for an interview.*

I have to stop myself
from laughing.

From saying, I was just there.

From asking if they'd seen
my baby brother
waiting in a cell.

> *Sure, sure,* I say.
> *Let's set that up.*

MY HEART SINKS

They must know.

THE SECOND CALL

I hang up.

The phone rings again.
Before I even get the chance
to calm my breath.

Hey, Zen.

> *Hey.*

I'm sorry, I say again.

> *Your brother, I get it—it's okay.*
> *I understand why you'd feel that way.*
> *But, Leo, one thing is really clear*
> *There's something bigger going on here.*

I hear Zen's breath
on the line.
In.
Out.

She steadies herself
and continues.

> *Look,*
> *I heard your brother's friends*
> *planned to prank*
> *the Asian Cultural Club.*

Said they were tired
of everything going on
overseas.

They want someone to blame—

For our parents being gone? I ask.

Yeah. I guess.
But this,
it's serious, Leo.
People are scared.

I know.

I'm one of them.

BRAVE

Bravery
is when you do
what is right
what is needed
despite the doubt
that eats at your insides.

THERE ARE TWO WAYS
TO DEAL WITH FEAR

One:
You let it win.
It crawls inside your brain,
sets up roadblocks,
freezes your feet in place.

Two:
You fight back.
Fists raised, teeth bared,
heart a drum in your chest.

Either way
it will force you to
decide.

WHAT I DECIDE TO DO

Pull fear out by the tail.

Stare it down.

Tell it there isn't
room enough
for both of us.

Get on my bike and
ride down
to the station.

FIRSTBORN

I step into the garage
as Dad's car pulls into
the driveway.

Early.
He's never home early.
But also, I can't believe
he went to work today.

He stops the car and
opens his door.

Dad.
      Son.

We stand.
Me in the doorway
Him half out of the car.

I wonder.
When he looks at me,
what does he see?

Leo.
The responsible one.
Leo.
The dependable one.

On my honor
I will do my best
to do my duty.

Leo? Dad says.

Yeah?

You doing okay, son?

UNANSWERED

Dad and I ride
to the station.

Words sit on my tongue
like wet clay.

I want to tell him about
the academy interview.

About ranking into Eagle
and ideas for my project.

I want to ask him
if he's proud of me.

TRUST ME

When we arrive,
I ask Dad to let me
talk to Jack first.

No problem,
I trust you, he says.
Think you can fix this?

Leo.
The reliable one.

HOW...

The clerk at the front desk
tells me they've moved Jack.
He's in the next building over.

A holding cell
for at-risk juveniles.

At risk.

How did the little kid
who used to race toy cars
around the family room
get here?

...DID WE GET HERE?

If only I knew how to stop you
from falling down this fateful path.
I'd hold your hand so tightly.
You'd beg me to let go.
Try to walk away.
I can't let you
live this way
anymore.

MOVING FORWARD

Dad and I walk to the holding center.
Show our IDs.
Wait in the lobby.

Listen to the clock.
tick
tick
tick
An endless song.

A woman calls us back.
One at a time, please, she says.
Dad nods.
I follow her.

Jack sits in a room alone.
He looks tired
and scared.
I want to hug him.

Instead I stand in the doorway.
Jack Attack, I whisper.
You okay, man?
The word feels strange on my tongue.

We are frozen in place.
       Yeah, he says finally.
       Can you bust me outta here?
       I didn't mean to—

I know, I say.
But we need to fix this.

WHAT JACK DOES

I expect him to be angry.
To lash out
and blame the others.

To tell me how
unfair it is
that Mom is gone.

And how he hates
everyone
responsible
for making her leave,
for putting her in danger.

I expect him to hate me
for being there.

For trying to convince him
to do the right thing
like I always do.

Instead
he stands up
walks over to me
puts his arms around my waist
and his head on my shoulder.

Thanks, man.

SOLIDARITY

A video camera
watches us
from across the room.

I hug my brother
tightly.

And try not to cry.

WHAT JACK SAYS

He tells me the truth.
What really happened
the night he snuck out.

How he met up
with the guys
from the support group.

Got high
and watched videos
of soldiers overseas.

How they started screaming
and swearing
until someone suggested
they blow 'em up.

I didn't have to ask who.

Jack stops at that part,
remembering Zen.

Your girlfriend, man,
I'm sorry.
I didn't even—

    She's not, I start to say.
    But yeah. Go on.

He tells me about the plan.

The lab.
The chemicals.

Some guy knew how to make
a bomb.

Just a joke, he says.
It was just a joke.
To scare them.

I want to tell him
how people could have been
hurt or
killed.

And how he should know
how serious schools
take this sort of threat.

But I bite my tongue.

Do you think the cops'll
let me go
if I confess?

I don't want to be a rat.

CLEAN

Physically strong.
Mentally awake.
Morally straight.

As if the lines
were perfectly clear,
and no one ever
had to step over them.

JUDGMENT

We sit around a long table.
Me and Dad on one side.
Jack on the other.

Next to him,
some guy in his 20s
who looks like he's already
tired of life.

At the end, an older woman.
She introduces herself:
a judge.
And the guy:
a youth advisor.
He asks who I am
and where is Jack's mother.

Dad explains.
The judge nods in the way
people do when you tell them
Mom is deployed.

It makes my stomach turn.

FEAR OF THE UNKNOWN

I want to hold my brother's hand
the way I did when we rode
our first roller coaster.

He wasn't the one
scared that day.

CONFESSION

Turns out
Jack doesn't
need to be
a rat.

The video cameras at school
caught the other boys standing around,
waiting for my brother
to do their dirty work.

The judge explains
the danger
and asks Jack
to make his plea.

Jack and I
make eye contact
across the table.
I nod my head.

His eyes look down.
He sighs deeply.
Like someone poked a hole
in a balloon.

Ma'am, he says.
I'm sorry.
And I want to make it up
to the school.

And those kids.
And my mom.

Mom doesn't even know yet.
Dad said he wanted
to wait until
the ruling.

Jack bites his bottom lip.
His hands shake.
He looks at me.
I nod a second time.

Me and my brother, Leo,
we got an idea.
We hope it'll make
things right.

He passes her the paper.
She puts on glasses,
clears her throat,
and reads our words.

The room is as quiet
as a snowstorm.

I stare into my lap
and pray.

STEPPING STONES

The judge looks at Jack.
Young man, she says.
You are at a crossroads.
Do you know what that means?

Your anger
can take you down a path
of hate and crime.
But what is to be gained from that?

You will only end up
hurting others,
yourself,
and your family.

It seems to me
that your brother here
looks out for you.
Don't shut him out.

Don't shut out
the people
who want to keep you
on the right road.

As she speaks,
I think about the stones in my path.
About how life tries
to stop you.

Tries to stop you
with floods,
with moss-covered rocks.
Tries to make you slip.

About how sometimes
we need
to set down
new stones.

And sometimes
we can't survive life's floods
without the people we love
holding our hands.

THE DECISION

The judge finishes her speech.
Adjusts her glasses,
and signs Jack's forms.

Dad thanks her
for understanding.
We all shake hands.

When she gets to me, she says,
Leo Solis.
A fine young man
looking after your brother like that.

I expect great things from you.

I feel the added weight
on my shoulders.

She grips my hand.
Shakes it firmly, then lets it fall,
sweaty, by my side.

Don't let life's burdens
pull you under.

And remember,
we are not on this road
alone.

SECOND IN COMMAND

Me and Jack
on the couch
side by side.

Focused.
In the zone.

It feels good to be together.
But I know I can't always be
the one to fix things.
I have to lean on him too.

Jack Attack, I say.
My Eagle project.
I'm gonna need some help, right?

He nods.

I need you to lead the crew.

Pauses the game.

> *Don't worry.*
> *I got your back, man.*

ON SUNDAY

Dad makes pancakes.

Reina stands on her stool next to him.
Fills each one
with smiley faces
made from chocolate chips.

Jack slices melon.
I fill coffee cups
and juice glasses.
We are a team.

We set a place for Mom
and call her on dad's phone.

I smile when I see her face.
Dad explained what happened,
but Mom doesn't bring it up.

Instead she asks what's for dinner.
Reina laughs (she doesn't understand
time zones) and puts a pancake
on Mom's plate.

We miss you, I say.
I think about the calendar,
each X closer to seeing her face
in person.

REVERENT

That morning in church
I think about what it means
to have faith.

To believe in God.
To believe in a higher purpose.
To believe in what's meant to be.

FORGIVENESS

Jack is released
on the grounds that he will
help with repairs at school
and make amends.
The others are in more serious trouble.

The judge agrees
that Jack's help on my Eagle project
fulfills his community service.
I draft my idea for review.

We invite Zen and her mom
to dinner.
Jack offers to cook.
The parents talk about
laundry
and bills
and other boring adult things.

We swap moving stories
and compare our favorite
places to live.

I like it here,
and think I might
come back
for college.

Zen smiles.
She wants to stay here, too.

We eat
and laugh.
And even though
our family puzzles
are missing a piece,
there is comfort
in what fills
the empty space.

THE ENVELOPE

It sits there.
On the counter.
My name typed
in straight black letters.

Mr. Leo Solis.

I am afraid to open it.

But I have learned a lot
about fear
and worry.

And I refuse to ever
let them win.

The envelope rips.
I read carefully.

You have been invited
to join the class
of summer academy students.

Invited.
To join.

My heart jumps.
I'm in.

SIX MONTHS LATER

The sky drizzles
familiar rain.

Red, white, and blue ribbon
weaves its way around benches
that form a circle.

A lone tree in the center.

The plaque below
dedicates the space
to the men and women
who fight for our freedom.

I stand nervously.
Scissors at the ready.

Our scoutmaster scans the crowd.
Boys from the troop,
some with their families.
Zen and her mom.
Other support group members.
Summer academy classmates.

Looks like you brought
the community together, Dad says.

Everything looks great.
This space—it's the perfect way
to honor local veterans.
And to unite everyone.

He pats my back
then pulls me into him
for a hug.

Your mom would be proud,
he says into my ear.
He releases the hug
but keeps hold of my shoulders.

We look at each other
and I see strength
underneath his sadness.

And something else.

He smiles.

I'm proud of you, son.

FOREVER THANKFUL

Jack is by my side
as I cut the ribbon,
dedicating the park
to the men and women who serve.

Dad and Reina sit in the front row.
I wish Mom had made it home
to see this.

A group of people
walk toward our site.
I wonder if they've come
to protest
or are just curious.

The crowd turns to watch.
I feel my heart race.
The group walks closer.
And in the center
wearing her uniform
and a huge smile,

Mom.

WANT TO KEEP READING?

If you liked this book, check out another book
from West 44 Books:

ONE TOO MANY LIES
L.A BOWEN

ISBN: 9781538382493

THE PHOTO

Myself in the middle.
All glasses
and long brown hair.

Kate on my right.
With bright blue eyes
and perfect makeup, as usual.

Abby to my left.
Her blonde hair, always changing,
had a pink streak that week.

The photo is cropped close
to hide the background.
What can't be seen,
a party...

Kate's Sweet 16!

I lied when my parents asked
if there was alcohol.

I wasn't the one drinking it.
Honest!

Either way
Mom and Dad
would not
approve.

Check out more books at:
www.west44books.com

An imprint of Enslow Publishing

WEST **44** BOOKS™

ABOUT THE AUTHOR

Sandi Van is a writer, counselor, and former special education teacher from Buffalo, New York. Her nonfiction piece, "Labor and Delivery" was featured in *Adoptive Families* magazine and her poetry won recognition in the Elmira *Star-Gazette* and the PennWriters' In Other Words contest. Sandi is a Navy wife and has witnessed the struggles families face when a parent is deployed. Her book is inspired by and dedicated to those families.